Roscoe
and the
Pelican
Rescue

Lynn ROWE REED

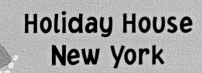

Holiday House
New York

*To all the people who helped
save the Gulf Coast wildlife*

The publisher wishes to thank
Jay Holcomb, Executive Director
of the International Bird Rescue
Research Center, for reviewing
this book for accuracy.

Printed and Bound in December 2010 at Kwong Fat Offset
Printing Co., Ltd., Dongguan City, China.
The text typeface is Jacoby.
The artwork was created with acrylic paint on canvas.
www.holidayhouse.com
First Edition
1 3 5 7 9 10 8 6 4 2

Library of Congress Cataloging-in-Publication Data
is available.
ISBN 978-0-8234-2352-1

Summer is my favorite time. I catch lightning bugs, eat s'mores, stay up late, and listen to cicadas chirping outside my window.

This will be my best summer ever. Tomorrow I'm taking a plane all by myself to visit my cousin Addison on the Gulf Coast.

Uncle Willie is a fisherman, and Aunt Olivia works in a veterinarian's office. They have one kid—my favorite cousin, Addison—and a new golden retriever named Roscoe.

The Atlantic Ocean is the second largest of the earth's four oceans and the most heavily traveled.

I can't stop talking about the ocean. Mom says *she* could use a vacation too—to get away from all the gloomy news. She tells me to pack lightly. It is so hard to sleep. The next morning, I'm ready to go at 5:34 a.m., and Mom is ready a few hours later.

During the flight I draw fish, calculate the ocean's temperatures, explain snorkeling to the man next to me, organize my lures, and practice holding my breath underwater.

In the terminal, big Uncle Willie is easy to find with his booming chuckle. Aunt Olivia smothers me with cherry red lipstick kisses.

At first Addison and I are quiet, but soon we chatter nonstop—all the way to her house.

Addison and I make a list of things to do in the morning.

(1) Swim (all strokes)
(2) snorkel
(3) build sand castle
(4) look for dolphin
(5) collect shells
(6) teach Roscoe to fetch
    stick from water
(7) turn somersaults
    in water
(8) fish/practice casting
(9) feed a fish to pelican
(10) play water volleyball

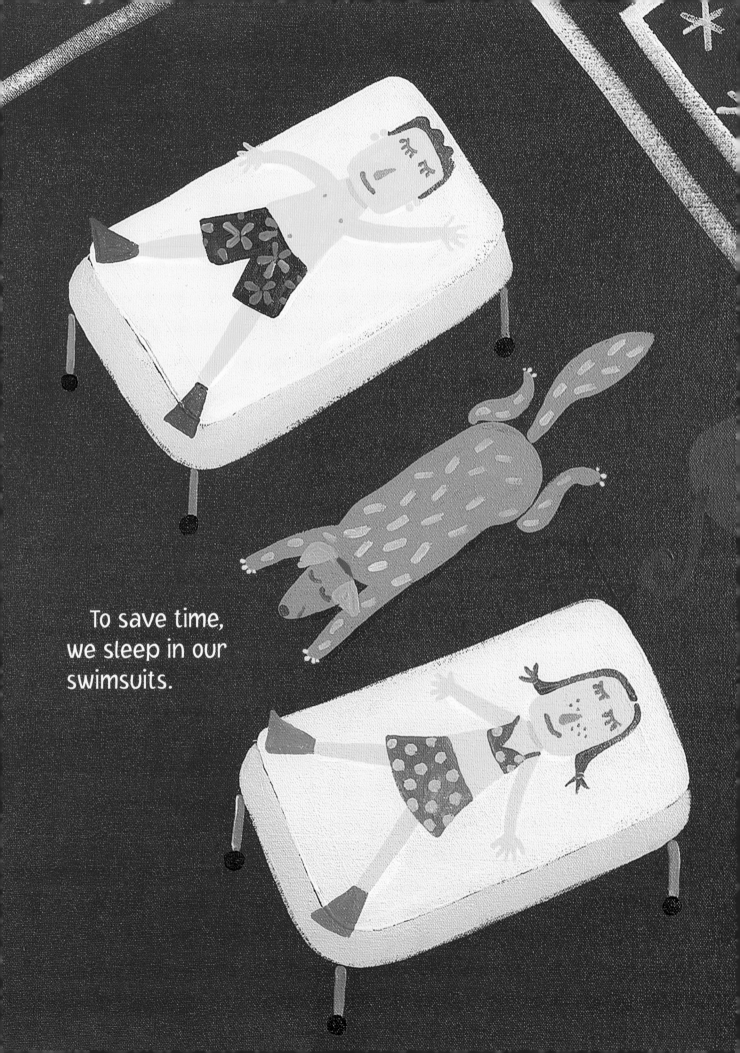

To save time,
we sleep in our
swimsuits.

The next morning
Addison and I race our
bikes to the beach.
Roscoe wins, of course!

At the water's edge, a big sign reads BEACH CLOSED. I can't imagine _why_ until I see brown balls of goo mixed in with the sand. When I peer closer, I see shrimp and hermit crabs that look as if they're covered in peanut butter!

The water looks really weird and smells funny. I wonder if this has to do with the story on the news about the big oil leak a month ago.

Roscoe takes off and then returns,
barking and running in circles. Addison
and I follow him to a clump on the beach.
   "Oh no," I tell Addison. "Roscoe found a dead bird."
But then I see that it's a pelican, and it's alive!
   "We need to get Aunt Olivia and Uncle Willie!" I say.

By the time we get back, Roscoe has found two more pelicans.
"I didn't think it would get this far!" growls Uncle Willie. His jaw is clenched and quivering in a way that scares me.

Aunt Olivia puts on gloves, scoops up the birds, and orders all of us into the truck. Uncle Willie drives past marshes and into town to the wildlife rescue place just down the road. Aunt Olivia and Uncle Willie have both trained there and know exactly how to care for the pelicans.

Latisha LaRoche meets us and puts the pelicans in a special room where they will eat and rest for a few days under a heat lamp. She wants to make sure the birds are strong enough to be cleaned.

The pelicans look so pitiful, my Adam's
apple starts to hurt like it does when
I'm trying hard not to cry.

On the day of the cleaning, Addison and I carry supplies to the shampoo room. Then Latisha puts a pelican in the sink, where Aunt Olivia suds it up, just like it's getting a shampoo. She even cleans inside the pelican's pouch.

Latisha and Aunt Olivia
clean each bird one by one.
Uncle Willie
rinses each one
until the water
runs clear. It takes
all afternoon to clean
the three pelicans.
Roscoe gets a
bath, too, while
Addison and
I wait!

The clean, wet pelicans are placed in front of large dryers. Even Roscoe wants to be dried. Before long they are clean and beautiful again!

Over the next few days, people nearby hear about our rescue and call Latisha so she can pick up more oil-covered animals. We all end up staying to help, even Uncle Willie. "I won't be catching fish anytime soon," he says.

Addison and I run errands with Roscoe while the adults clean eleven pelicans, four turtles, and two otters. "Maybe we should give Roscoe another name," says Addison. "I vote for Rescue!"

When the work is done, Latisha tags each animal with a number so it can be tracked later.

"Now what will we do with all these animals?" I ask Uncle Willie. "We can't take them back to that nasty water!"

"I have an idea," he says with a wink.

Aunt Olivia packs the truck and we drive west, toward Texas.

After a few hours, Uncle Willie pulls over and we walk to the beach, toting all of our new friends. Addison and I search for water calm and blue.

"Okay, Sport," says Uncle Willie. "You have one day of vacation left. What are you waiting for?"

It's the best day of my summer vacation—ever!

On April 20, 2010, the drilling platform Deepwater
Horizon exploded in the Gulf of Mexico, resulting in the
worst ecological disaster in United States history.

In the following six months, more than 665 birds
were rescued from the water and cleaned. They were
then tagged with a federal ID number and released in
cleaner areas in the Gulf.

Thousands of people worked to clean animals along
the Gulf Coast. Without those people, many animals
would not have survived this disaster.